The Village and The Newspaper

George Crabbe

Table of Contents

The Village and The Newspaper

George Crabbe

THE VILLAGE

BOOK I.—THE ARGUMENT.

The Subject proposed—Remarks upon Pastoral Poetry—A Tract of Country near the Coast described—An Impoverished Borough—Smugglers and their Assistants—Rude Manners of the Inhabitants—Ruinous Effects of the High Tide—The Village Life more generally considered: Evils of it—The Youthful Labourer—The Old Man: his Soliloquy—The Parish Workhouse: its Inhabitants—The sick Poor: their Apothecary—The dying Pauper—The Village Priest.

The Village and The Newspaper

The Village Life, and every care that reigns
O'er youthful peasants and declining swains;
What labour yields, and what, that labour past,
Age, in its hour of languor, finds at last;
What form the real Picture of the Poor,
Demand a song—the Muse can give no more.
   Fled are those times, when, in harmonious strains,
The rustic poet praised his native plains:
No Shepherds now, in smooth alternate verse,
Their country's beauty or their nymphs rehearse;
Yet still for these we frame the tender strain,
Still in our lays fond Corydons complain,
And shepherds' boys their amorous pains reveal,
The only pains, alas! they never feel.
   On Mincio's banks, in Caesar's bounteous reign,
If Tityrus found the Golden Age again,
Must sleepy bards the nattering dream prolong,
Mechanic echoes of the Mantuan song?
From Truth and Nature shall we widely stray,
Where Virgil, not where Fancy, leads the way?
   Yes, thus the Muses sing of happy swains,
Because the Muses never knew their pains:
They boast their peasant's pipes; but peasants now
Resign their pipes and plod behind the plough;
And few, amid the rural tribe, have time
To number syllables and play with rhyme;
Save honest DUCK, what son of verse could share
The poet's rapture and the peasant's care?
Or the great labours of the field degrade,
With the new peril of a poorer trade?
   From this chief cause these idle praises spring,
That themes so easy few forbear to sing;
For no deep thought the trifling subjects ask;
To sing of shepherds is an easy task:
The happy youth assumes the common strain,

The Village and The Newspaper

A nymph his mistress, and himself a swain;
With no sad scenes he clouds his tuneful prayer,
But all, to look like her, is painted fair.
   I grant indeed that fields and flocks have charms
For him that grazes or for him that farms;
But when amid such pleasing scenes I trace
The poor laborious natives of the place,
And see the mid–day sun, with fervid ray,
On their bare heads and dewy temples play;
While some, with feebler heads and fainter hearts,
Deplore their fortune, yet sustain their parts
Then shall I dare these real ills to hide
In tinsel trappings of poetic pride?
   No; cast by Fortune on a frowning coast,
Which neither groves nor happy valleys boast;
Where other cares than those the Muse relates,
And other shepherds dwell with other mates;
By such examples taught, I paint the Cot,
As Truth will paint it, and as Bards will not:
Nor you, ye Poor, of letter'd scorn complain,
To you the smoothest song is smooth in vain;
O'ercome by labour, and bow'd down by time,
Feel you the barren flattery of a rhyme?
Can poets soothe you, when you pine for bread,
By winding myrtles round your ruin'd shed?
Can their light tales your weighty griefs o'erpower,
Or glad with airy mirth the toilsome hour?
   Lo! where the heath, with withering brake grown o'er,
Lends the light turf that warms the neighbouring poor;
From thence a length of burning sand appears,
Where the thin harvest waves its wither'd ears;
Rank weeds, that every art and care defy,
Reign o'er the land, and rob the blighted rye.
There thistles stretch their prickly arms afar,
And to the ragged infant threaten war;
There poppies nodding, mock the hope of toil,

The Village and The Newspaper

There the blue bugloss paints the sterile soil;
Hardy and high, above the slender sheaf,
The slimy mallow waves her silky leaf;
O'er the young shoot the charlock throws a shade,
And clasping tares cling round the sickly blade.
With mingled tints the rocky coasts abound,
And a sad splendour vainly shines around.
So looks the nymph whom wretched arts adorn,
Betray'd by man, then left for man to scorn;
Whose cheek in vain assumes the mimic rose,
While her sad eyes the troubled breast disclose;
Whose outward splendour is but folly's dress,
Exposing most, when most it gilds distress.

  Here joyless roam a wild amphibious race,
With sullen woe display'd in every face;
Who, far from civil arts and social fly,
And scowl at strangers with suspicious eye.

  Here too the lawless merchant of the main
Draws from his plough th' intoxicated swain;
Want only claim'd the labour of the day,
But vice now steals his nightly rest away.

  Where are the swains, who, daily labour done,
With rural games play'd down the setting sun;
Who struck with matchless force the bounding ball,
Or made the pond'rous quoit obliquely fall;
While some huge Ajax, terrible and strong,
Engaged some artful stripling of the throng.
And fell beneath him, foil'd, while far around
Hoarse triumph rose, and rocks return'd the sound?
Where now are these?—Beneath yon cliff they stand,
To show the freighted pinnace where to land;
To load the ready steed with guilty haste,
To fly in terror o'er the pathless waste,
Or, when detected, in their straggling course,
To foil their foes by cunning or by force;
Or, yielding part (which equal knaves demand),

4

The Village and The Newspaper

To gain a lawless passport through the land.
  Here, wand'ring long, amid these frowning fields,
I sought the simple life that Nature yields;
Rapine and Wrong and Fear usurp'd her place,
And a bold, artful, surly, savage race;
Who, only skill'd to take the finny tribe,
The yearly dinner, or septennial bribe,
Wait on the shore, and, as the waves run high,
On the tost vessel bend their eager eye,
Which to their coast directs its vent'rous way;
Theirs or the ocean's miserable prey.
  As on their neighbouring beach yon swallows stand,
And wait for favouring winds to leave the land;
While still for flight the ready wing is spread:
So waited I the favouring hour, and fled;
Fled from these shores where guilt and famine reign,
And cried, Ah! hapless they who still remain;
Who still remain to hear the ocean roar,
Whose greedy waves devour the lessening shore;
Till some fierce tide, with more imperious sway,
Sweeps the low hut and all it holds away;
When the sad tenant weeps from door to door;
And begs a poor protection from the poor!
  But these are scenes where Nature's niggard hand
Gave a spare portion to the famish'd land;
Hers is the fault, if here mankind complain
Of fruitless toil and labour spent in vain;
But yet in other scenes more fair in view,
When Plenty smiles—alas! she smiles for few –
And those who taste not, yet behold her store,
Are as the slaves that dig the golden ore –
The wealth around them makes them doubly poor.
Or will you deem them amply paid in health,
Labour's fair child, that languishes with wealth?
Go then! and see them rising with the sun,
Through a long course of daily toil to run;

The Village and The Newspaper

See them beneath the Dog–star's raging heat,
When the knees tremble and the temples beat;
Behold them, leaning on their scythes, look o'er
The labour past, and toils to come explore;
See them alternate suns and showers engage,
And hoard up aches and anguish for their age;
Through fens and marshy moors their steps pursue,
When their warm pores imbibe the evening dew;
Then own that labour may as fatal be
To these thy slaves, as thine excess to thee.
   Amid this tribe too oft a manly pride
Strives in strong toil the fainting heart to hide;
There may you see the youth of slender frame
Contend with weakness, weariness, and shame;
Yet, urged along, and proudly loth to yield,
He strives to join his fellows of the field:
Till long–contending nature droops at last,
Declining health rejects his poor repast,
His cheerless spouse the coming danger sees,
And mutual murmurs urge the slow disease.
   Yet grant them health, 'tis not for us to tell,
Though the head droops not, that the heart is well;
Or will you praise that homely, healthy fare,
Plenteous and plain, that happy peasants share?
Oh! trifle not with wants you cannot feel,
Nor mock the misery of a stinted meal;
Homely, not wholesome, plain, not plenteous, such
As you who praise would never deign to touch.
   Ye gentle souls, who dream of rural ease,
Whom the smooth stream and smoother sonnet please;
Go! if the peaceful cot your praises share,
Go look within, and ask if peace be there;
If peace be his, that drooping weary sire;
Or theirs, that offspring round their feeble fire;
Or hers, that matron pale, whose trembling hand
Turns on the wretched hearth th' expiring brand!

The Village and The Newspaper

Nor yet can Time itself obtain for these
Life's latest comforts, due respect and ease;
For yonder see that hoary swain, whose age
Can with no cares except its own engage;
Who, propt on that rude staff, looks up to see
The bare arms broken from the withering tree,
On which, a boy, he climb'd the loftiest bough,
Then his first joy, but his sad emblem now.
  He once was chief in all the rustic trade;
His steady hand the straightest furrow made;
Full many a prize he won, and still is proud
To find the triumphs of his youth allow'd;
A transient pleasure sparkles in his eyes,
He hears and smiles, then thinks again and sighs:
For now he journeys to his grave in pain;
The rich disdain him; nay the poor disdain:
Alternate masters now their slave command,
Urge the weak efforts of his feeble hand,
And, when his age attempts its task in vain,
With ruthless taunts, of lazy poor complain.
  Oft may you see him, when he tends the sheep,
His winter charge, beneath the hillock weep;
Oft hear him murmur to the winds that blow
O'er his white locks and bury them in snow,
When, rous'd by rage and muttering in the morn,
He mends the broken hedge with icy thorn: –
  "Why do I live, when I desire to be
At once from life and life's long labour free?
Like leaves in spring, the young are blown away,
Without the sorrows of a slow decay;
I, like yon withered leaf remain behind,
Nipt by the frost, and shivering in the wind;
There it abides till younger buds come on
As I, now all my fellow–swains are gone,
Then from the rising generation thrust,
It falls, like me, unnoticed to the dust.

The Village and The Newspaper

"These fruitful fields, these numerous flocks I see,
Are others' gain, but killing cares to me;
To me the children of my youth are lords,
Cool in their looks, but hasty in their words:
Wants of their own demand their care; and who
Feels his own want and succours others too?
A lonely, wretched man, in pain I go,
None need my help, and none relieve my woe;
Then let my bones beneath the turf be laid,
And men forget the wretch they would not aid."
   Thus groan the old, till by disease oppress'd,
They taste a final woe, and then they rest.
   Theirs is yon House that holds the parish poor,
Whose walls of mud scarce bear the broken door;
There, where the putrid vapours, flagging, play,
And the dull wheel hums doleful through the day;—
There children dwell who know no parents' care;
Parents, who know no children's love, dwell there!
Heart—broken matrons on their joyless bed,
Forsaken wives, and mothers never wed;
Dejected widows with unheeded tears,
And crippled age with more than childhood fears;
The lame, the blind, and, far the happiest they!
The moping idiot, and the madman gay.
   Here too the sick their final doom receive,
Here brought, amid the scenes of grief, to grieve,
Where the loud groans from some sad chamber flow,
Mixt with the clamours of the crowd below;
Here, sorrowing, they each kindred sorrow scan,
And the cold charities of man to man:
Whose laws indeed for ruin'd age provide,
And strong compulsion plucks the scrap from pride;
But still that scrap is bought with many a sigh,
And pride embitters what it can't deny.
Say, ye, opprest by some fantastic woes,
Some jarring nerve that baffles your repose;

The Village and The Newspaper

Who press the downy couch, while slaves advance
With timid eye to read the distant glance;
Who with sad prayers the weary doctor tease,
To name the nameless ever new disease;
Who with mock patience dire complaints endure,
Which real pain and that alone can cure;
How would ye bear in real pain to lie,
Despised, neglected, left alone to die?
How would ye bear to draw your latest breath
Where all that's wretched paves the way for death?
 Such is that room which one rude beam divides,
And naked rafters form the sloping sides;
Where the vile bands that bind the thatch are seen,
And lath and mud are all that lie between;
Save one dull pane, that, coarsely patch'd, gives way
To the rude tempest, yet excludes the day:
Here, on a matted flock, with dust o'erspread,
The drooping wretch reclines his languid head;
For him no hand the cordial cup applies,
Or wipes the tear that stagnates in his eyes;
No friends with soft discourse his pain beguile,
Or promise hope, till sickness wears a smile.
 But soon a loud and hasty summons calls,
Shakes the thin roof, and echoes round the walls;
Anon, a figure enters, quaintly neat,
All pride and business, bustle and conceit;
With looks unalter'd by these scenes of woe,
With speed that, entering, speaks his haste to go,
He bids the gazing throng around him fly,
And carries fate and physic in his eye:
A potent quack, long versed in human ills,
Who first insults the victim whom he kills;
Whose murd'rous hand a drowsy Bench protect,
And whose most tender mercy is neglect.
 Paid by the parish for attendance here,
He wears contempt upon his sapient sneer;

The Village and The Newspaper

In haste he seeks the bed where Misery lies,
Impatience mark'd in his averted eyes;
And, some habitual queries hurried o'er,
Without reply, he rushes on the door:
His drooping patient, long inured to pain,
And long unheeded, knows remonstrance vain;
He ceases now the feeble help to crave
Of man; and silent sinks into the grave.
   But ere his death some pious doubts arise,
Some simple fears, which "bold bad" men despise;
Fain would he ask the parish priest to prove
His title certain to the joys above:
For this he sends the murmuring nurse, who calls
The holy stranger to these dismal walls:
And doth not he, the pious man, appear,
He, "passing rich, with forty pounds a year?"
Ah!no; a shepherd of a different stock,
And far unlike him, feeds this little flock:
A jovial youth, who thinks his Sunday's task
As much as God or man can fairly ask;
The rest he gives to loves and labours light,
To fields the morning, and to feasts the night;
None better skill'd the noisy pack to guide,
To urge their chase, to cheer them or to chide;
A sportsman keen, he shoots through half the day,
And, skill'd at whist, devotes the night to play:
Then, while such honours bloom around his head,
Shall he sit sadly by the sick man's bed,
To raise the hope he feels not, or with zeal
To combat fears that e'en the pious, feel?
   Now once again the gloomy scene explore,
Less gloomy now; the bitter hour is o'er,
The man of many sorrows sighs no more. –
Up yonder hill, behold how sadly slow
The bier moves winding from the vale below:
There lie the happy dead, from trouble free,

And the glad parish pays the frugal fee:
No more, O Death! thy victim starts to hear
Churchwarden stern, or kingly overseer;
No more the farmer claims his humble bow,
Thou art his lord, the best of tyrants thou!
   Now to the church behold the mourners come,
Sedately torpid and devoutly dumb;
The village children now their games suspend,
To see the bier that bears their ancient friend:
For he was one in all their idle sport,
And like a monarch ruled their little court;
The pliant bow he form'd, the flying ball,
The bat, the wicket, were his labours all;
Him now they follow to his grave, and stand,
Silent and sad, and gazing hand in hand;
While bending low, their eager eyes explore
The mingled relics of the parish poor.
The bell tolls late, the moping owl flies round,
Fear marks the flight and magnifies the sound;
The busy priest, detain'd by weightier care,
Defers his duty till the day of prayer;
And, waiting long, the crowd retire distrest,
To think a poor man's bones should lie unblest.

BOOK II—THE ARGUMENT.

There are found, amid the Evils of a laborious Life, some Views of Tranquillity and
Happiness—The Repose and Pleasure of a Summer Sabbath: interrupted by Intoxication
and Dispute—Village Detraction— Complaints of the 'Squire—The Evening
Riots—Justice—Reasons for this unpleasant View of Rustic Life: the Effect it should
have upon the Lower Classes; and the Higher—These last have their peculiar Distresses:
Exemplified in the Life and heroic Death of Lord Robert Manners—Concluding Address
to His Grace the Duke of Rutland.

No longer truth, though shown in verse, disdain,

The Village and The Newspaper

But own the Village Life a life of pain:
I too must yield, that oft amid those woes
Are gleams of transient mirth and hours of sweet repose,
Such as you find on yonder sportive Green,
The 'squire's tall gate and churchway–walk between;
Where loitering stray a little tribe of friends,
On a fair Sunday when the sermon ends:
Then rural beaux their best attire put on,
To win their nymphs, as other nymphs are won:
While those long wed go plain, and by degrees,
Like other husbands, quit their care to please.
Some of the sermon talk, a sober crowd,
And loudly praise, if it were preach'd aloud;
Some on the labours of the week look round,
Feel their own worth, and think their toil renown'd;
While some, whose hopes to no renown extend,
Are only pleased to find their labours end.
  Thus, as their hours glide on, with pleasure fraught
Their careful masters brood the painful thought;
Much in their mind they murmur and lament,
That one fair day should be so idly spent;
And think that Heaven deals hard, to tithe their store
And tax their time for preachers and the poor.
  Yet still, ye humbler friends, enjoy your hour,
This is your portion, yet unclaim'd of power;
This is Heaven's gift to weary men oppress'd,
And seems the type of their expected rest:
But yours, alas! are joys that soon decay;
Frail joys, begun and ended with the day;
Or yet, while day permits those joys to reign,
The village vices drive them from the plain.
  See the stout churl, in drunken fury great,
Strike the bare bosom of his teeming mate!
His naked vices, rude and unrefined,
Exert their open empire o'er the mind;
But can we less the senseless rage despise,

The Village and The Newspaper

Because the savage acts without disguise?
  Yet here Disguise, the city's vice, is seen,
And Slander steals along and taints the Green:
At her approach domestic peace is gone,
Domestic broils at her approach come on;
She to the wife the husband's crime conveys,
She tells the husband when his consort strays;
Her busy tongue, through all the little state,
Diffuses doubt, suspicion, and debate;
Peace, tim'rous goddess! quits her old domain,
In sentiment and song content to reign.
  Nor are the nymphs that breathe the rural air
So fair as Cynthia's, nor so chaste as fair:
These to the town afford each fresher face,
And the clown's trull receives the peer's embrace;
From whom, should chance again convey her down,
The peer's disease in turn attacks the clown.
  Here too the 'squire, or 'squire–like farmer, talk,
How round their regions nightly pilferers walk;
How from their ponds the fish are borne, and all
The rip'ning treasures from their lofty wall;
How meaner rivals in their sports delight,
Just right enough to claim a doubtful right;
Who take a licence round their fields to stray,
A mongrel race! the poachers of the day.
  And hark! the riots of the Green begin,
That sprang at first from yonder noisy inn;
What time the weekly pay was vanish'd all,
And the slow hostess scored the threat'ning wall;
What time they ask'd, their friendly feast to close,
A final cup, and that will make them foes;
When blows ensue that break the arm of toil,
And rustic battle ends the boobies' broil.
  Save when to yonder Hall they bend their way,
Where the grave Justice ends the grievous fray;
He who recites, to keep the poor in awe,

The Village and The Newspaper

The law's vast volume—for he knows the law: –
To him with anger or with shame repair
The injured peasant and deluded fair.
  Lo! at his throne the silent nymph appears,
Frail by her shape, but modest in her tears;
And while she stands abash'd, with conscious eye,
Some favourite female of her judge glides by,
Who views with scornful glance the strumpet's fate,
And thanks the stars that made her keeper great:
Near her the swain, about to bear for life
One certain evil, doubts 'twixt war and wife;
But, while the faltering damsel takes her oath,
Consents to wed, and so secures them both.
  Yet why, you ask, these humble crimes relate,
Why make the Poor as guilty as the Great?
To show the great, those mightier sons of pride,
How near in vice the lowest are allied;
Such are their natures and their passions such,
But these disguise too little, those too much:
So shall the man of power and pleasure see
In his own slave as vile a wretch as he;
In his luxurious lord the servant find
His own low pleasures and degenerate mind:
And each in all the kindred vices trace,
Of a poor, blind, bewilder'd erring race,
Who, a short time in varied fortune past,
Die, and are equal in the dust at last.
  And you, ye Poor, who still lament your fate,
Forbear to envy those you call the Great;
And know, amid those blessings they possess,
They are, like you, the victims of distress;
While Sloth, with many a pang torments her slave,
Fear waits on guilt, and Danger shakes the brave.
  Oh! if in life one noble chief appears,
Great in his name, while blooming in his years;
Born to enjoy whate'er delights mankind,

The Village and The Newspaper

And yet to all you feel or fear resign'd;
Who gave up joys and hopes to you unknown,
For pains and dangers greater than your own:
If such there be, then let your murmurs cease,
Think, think of him, and take your lot in peace.
And such there was:—Oh! grief, that checks our pride,
Weeping we say there was, for MANNERS {1} died:
Beloved of Heaven, these humble lines forgive
That sing of Thee, and thus aspire to live.
   As the tall oak, whose vigorous branches form
An ample shade, and brave the wildest storm,
High o'er the subject wood is seen to grow,
The guard and glory of the trees below;
Till on its head the fiery bolt descends,
And o'er the plain the shattered trunk extends;
Yet then it lies, all wond'rous as before,
And still the glory, though the guard no more:
   So THOU, when every virtue, every grace,
Rose in thy soul, or shone within thy face;
When, though the son of GRANBY, thou wert known
Less by thy father's glory than thy own;
When Honour loved and gave thee every charm,
Fire to thy eye and vigour to thy arm;
Then from our lofty hopes and longing eyes,
Fate and thy virtues call'd thee to the skies;
Yet still we wonder at thy tow'ring fame,
And, losing thee, still dwell upon thy name.
   Oh! ever honour'd, ever valued! say,
What verse can praise thee, or what work repay?
Yet verse (in all we can) thy worth repays,
Nor trusts the tardy zeal of future days: –
Honours for thee thy country shall prepare,
Thee in their hearts, the good, the brave shall bear;
To deeds like thine shall noblest chiefs aspire,
The Muse shall mourn thee, and the world admire.
   In future times, when smit with Glory's charms,

The untried youth first quits a father's arms; –
"Oh! be like him," the weeping sire shall say;
"Like MANNERS walk, who walk'd in Honour's way;
In danger foremost, yet in death sedate,
Oh! be like him in all things, but his fate!"
    If for that fate such public tears be shed,
That Victory seems to die now THOU art dead;
How shall a friend his nearer hope resign,
That friend a brother, and whose soul was thine?
By what bold lines shall we his grief express,
Or by what soothing numbers make it less?
    'Tis not, I know, the chiming of a song,
Nor all the powers that to the Muse belong,
Words aptly cull'd, and meaning well express'd,
Can calm the sorrows of a wounded breast;
But Virtue, soother of the fiercest pains,
Shall heal that bosom, RUTLAND, where she reigns.
    Yet hard the task to heal the bleeding heart,
To bid the still–recurring thoughts depart,
Tame the fierce grief and stem the rising sigh,
And curb rebellious passion, with reply;
Calmly to dwell on all that pleased before,
And yet to know that all shall please no more; –
Oh! glorious labour of the soul, to save
Her captive powers, and bravely mourn the brave.
    To such these thoughts will lasting comfort give –
Life is not measured by the time we live:
'Tis not an even course of threescore years, –
A life of narrow views and paltry fears,
Gray hairs and wrinkles, and the cares they bring,
That take from Death the terrors or the sting;
But 'tis the gen'rous spirit, mounting high
Above the world, that native of the sky;
The noble spirit, that, in dangers brave
Calmly looks on, or looks beyond the grave: –
Such MANNERS was, so he resign'd his breath,

If in a glorious, then a timely death.
  Cease, then, that grief, and let those tears subside;
If Passion rule us, be that passion pride;
If Reason, reason bids us strive to raise
Our fallen hearts, and be like him we praise;
Or if Affection still the soul subdue,
Bring all his virtues, all his worth in view,
And let Affection find its comfort too:
For how can Grief so deeply wound the heart,
When Admiration claims so large a part?
  Grief is a foe—expel him then thy soul;
Let nobler thoughts the nearer views control!
Oh! make the age to come thy better care,
See other RUTLANDS, other GRANBYS there!
And, as thy thoughts through streaming ages glide,
See other heroes die as MANNERS died:
And from their fate, thy race shall nobler grow,
As trees shoot upwards that are pruned below;
Or as old Thames, borne down with decent pride,
Sees his young streams run warbling at his side;
Though some, by art cut off, no longer run,
And some are lost beneath the summer sun –
Yet the pure stream moves on, and, as it moves,
Its power increases and its use improves;
While plenty round its spacious waves bestow,
Still it flows on, and shall for ever flow.

THE NEWSPAPER

E quibus, hi vacuas implent sermonibus aures:
Hi narrata ferunt alio; mensuraque ficti
Crescit, et auditis aliquid novus adjicit auctor:
Illic Credulitas, illic temerarius Error,
Vanaque Laetitia est, consternatique Timores,
Seditioque repens, dubioque auctore Susurri.

The Village and The Newspaper

OVID, Metamorphoses

THE ARGUMENT

This not a Time favourable to Poetical Composition: and why— Newspapers enemies to Literature, and their general Influence—Their Numbers—The Sunday Monitor—Their general Character—Their Effect upon Individuals—upon Society—in the Country—The Village Freeholder—What Kind of Composition a Newspaper is; and the Amusement it affords—Of what Parts it is chiefly composed—Articles of Intelligence: Advertisements: The Stage: Quacks: Puffing—The Correspondents to a Newspaper, political and poetical—Advice to the latter—Conclusion.

A time like this, a busy, bustling time,
Suits ill with writers, very ill with rhyme:
Unheard we sing, when party–rage runs strong,
And mightier madness checks the flowing song:
Or, should we force the peaceful Muse to wield
Her feeble arms amid the furious field,
Where party–pens a wordy war maintain,
Poor is her anger, and her friendship vain;
And oft the foes who feel her sting, combine,
Till serious vengeance pays an idle line:
For party–poets are like wasps, who dart
Death to themselves, and to their foes but smart.
  Hard then our fate: if general themes we choose,
Neglect awaits the song, and chills the Muse;
Or should we sing the subject of the day,
To–morrow's wonder puffs our praise away.
More blest the bards of that poetic time,
When all found readers who could find a rhyme;
Green grew the bays on every teeming head,
And Cibber was enthroned, and Settle read.
Sing, drooping Muse, the cause of thy decline;
Why reign no more the once–triumphant Nine?
Alas! new charms the wavering many gain,

The Village and The Newspaper

And rival sheets the reader's eye detain;
A daily swarm, that banish every Muse,
Come flying forth, and mortals call them NEWS:
For these, unread, the noblest volumes lie;
For these, in sheets unsoil'd, the Muses die;
Unbought, unblest, the virgin copies wait
In vain for fame, and sink, unseen, to fate.

Since, then, the Town forsakes us for our foes,
The smoothest numbers for the harshest prose;
Let us, with generous scorn, the taste deride,
And sing our rivals with a rival's pride.

Ye gentle poets, who so oft complain
That foul neglect is all your labours gain;
That pity only checks your growing spite
To erring man, and prompts you still to write;
That your choice works on humble stalls are laid,
Or vainly grace the windows of the trade;
Be ye my friends, if friendship e'er can warm
Those rival bosoms whom the Muses charm;
Think of the common cause wherein we go,
Like gallant Greeks against the Trojan foe;
Nor let one peevish chief his leader blame,
Till, crown'd with conquest, we regain our fame;
And let us join our forces to subdue
This bold assuming but successful crew.

I sing of NEWS, and all those vapid sheets
The rattling hawker vends through gaping streets;
Whate'er their name, whate'er the time they fly,
Damp from the press, to charm the reader's eye:
For soon as Morning dawns with roseate hue,
The HERALD of the morn arises too;
POST after POST succeeds, and, all day long,
GAZETTES and LEDGERS swarm, a noisy throng.
When evening comes, she comes with all her train;
Of LEDGERS, CHRONICLES, and POSTS again.
Like bats, appearing when the sun goes down,

From holes obscure and corners of the town.
Of all these triflers, all like these, I write;
Oh! like my subject could my song delight,
The crowd at Lloyd's one poet's name should raise,
And all the Alley echo to his praise.

   In shoals the hours their constant numbers bring,
Like insects waking to th' advancing spring;
Which take their rise from grubs obscene that lie
In shallow pools, or thence ascend the sky:
Such are these base ephemeras, so born
To die before the next revolving morn.
Yet thus they differ: insect—tribes are lost
In the first visit of a winters frost;
While these remain, a base but constant breed,
Whose swarming sons their short—lived sires succeed;
No changing season makes their number less,
Nor Sunday shines a sabbath on the press!

   Then lo! the sainted MONITOR is born,
Whose pious face some sacred texts adorn:
As artful sinners cloak the secret sin,
To veil with seeming grace the guile within;
So moral Essays on his front appear,
But all is carnal business in the rear;
The fresh—coin'd lie, the secret whisper'd last,
And all the gleanings of the six days past.

   With these retired through half the Sabbath—day,
The London lounger yawns his hours away:
Not so, my little flock! your preacher fly,
Nor waste the time no worldly wealth can buy;
But let the decent maid and sober clown
Pray for these idlers of the sinful town:
This day, at least, on nobler themes bestow,
Nor give to WOODFALL, or the world below.

   But, Sunday past, what numbers flourish then,
What wondrous labours of the press and pen;
Diurnal most, some thrice each week affords,

The Village and The Newspaper

Some only once,—O avarice of words!
When thousand starving minds such manna seek,
To drop the precious food but once a week.
   Endless it were to sing the powers of all,
Their names, their numbers; how they rise and fall:
Like baneful herbs the gazer's eye they seize,
Rush to the head, and poison where they please:
Like idle flies, a busy, buzzing train,
They drop their maggots in the trifler's brain:
That genia soil receives the fruitful store,
And there they grow, and breed a thousand more.
   Now be their arts display'd, how first they choose
A cause and party, as the bard his Muse;
Inspired by these, with clamorous zeal they cry,
And through the town their dreams and omens fly;
So the Sibylline leaves were blown about,
Disjointed scraps of fate involved in doubt;
So idle dreams, the journals of the night,
Are right and wrong by turns, and mingle wrong with right.—
Some champions for the rights that prop the crown,
Some sturdy patriots, sworn to pull them down;
Some neutral powers, with secret forces fraught,
Wishing for war, but willing to be bought:
While some to every side and party go,
Shift every friend, and join with every foe;
Like sturdy rogues in privateers, they strike
This side and that, the foes of both alike;
A traitor—crew, who thrive in troubled times,
Fear'd for their force, and courted for their crimes.
   Chief to the prosperous side the numbers sail,
Fickle and false, they veer with every gale;
As birds that migrate from a freezing shore
In search of warmer climes, come skimming o'er,
Some bold adventurers first prepare to try
The doubtful sunshine of the distant sky;
But soon the growing Summer's certain sun

The Village and The Newspaper

Wins more and more, till all at last are won:
So, on the early prospect of disgrace,
Fly in vast troops this apprehensive race;
Instinctive tribes! their failing food they dread,
And buy, with timely change, their future bread.

   Such are our guides; how many a peaceful head,
Born to be still, have they to wrangling led!
How many an honest zealot stol'n from trade,
And factious tools of pious pastors made!
With clews like these they thread the maze of state,
These oracles explore, to learn our fate;
Pleased with the guides who can so well deceive,
Who cannot lie so fast as they believe.

   Oft lend I, loth, to some sage friend an ear,
(For we who will not speak are doom'd to hear);
While he, bewilder'd, tells his anxious thought,
Infectious fear from tainted scribblers caught,
Or idiot hope; for each his mind assails,
As LLOYD'S court–light or STOCKDALE'S gloom prevails.
Yet stand I patient while but one declaims,
Or gives dull comments on the speech he maims:
But oh! ye Muses, keep your votary's feet
From tavern–haunts where politicians meet;
Where rector, doctor, and attorney pause,
First on each parish, then each public cause:
Indited roads, and rates that still increase;
The murmuring poor, who will not fast in peace;
Election zeal and friendship, since declined;
A tax commuted, or a tithe in kind;
The Dutch and Germans kindling into strife;
Dull port and poachers vile; the serious ills of life.

   Here comes the neighbouring Justice, pleased to guide
His little club, and in the chair preside.
In private business his commands prevail,
On public themes his reasoning turns the scale;
Assenting silence soothes his happy ear,

The Village and The Newspaper

And, in or out, his party triumphs here.
   Nor here th' infectious rage for party stops,
But flits along from palaces to shops;
Our weekly journals o'er the land abound,
And spread their plague and influenzas round;
The village, too, the peaceful, pleasant plain,
Breeds the Whig farmer and the Tory swain;
Brookes' and St Alban's boasts not, but, instead,
Stares the Red Ram, and swings the Rodney's Head:−
Hither, with all a patriot's care, comes he
Who owns the little hut that makes him free;
Whose yearly forty shillings buy the smile
Of mightier men, and never waste the while;
Who feels his freehold's worth, and looks elate,
A little prop and pillar of the state.
   Here he delights the weekly news to con,
And mingle comments as he blunders on;
To swallow all their varying authors teach,
To spell a title, and confound a speech:
Till with a muddled mind he quits the news,
And claims his nation's licence to abuse;
Then joins the cry, "That all the courtly race
Are venal candidates for power and place;"
Yet feels some joy, amid the general vice,
That his own vote will bring its wonted price.
   These are the ills the teeming Press supplies,
The pois'nous springs from learning's fountain rise;
Not there the wise alone their entrance find,
Imparting useful light to mortals blind;
But, blind themselves, these erring guides hold out
Alluring lights to lead us far about;
Screen'd by such means, here Scandal whets her quill,
Here Slander shoots unseen, whene'er she will;
Here Fraud and Falsehood labour to deceive,
And Folly aids them both, impatient to believe.
Such, sons of Britain! are the guides ye trust;

The Village and The Newspaper

So wise their counsel, their reports so just!–
Yet, though we cannot call their morals pure,
Their judgment nice, or their decisions sure;
Merit they have to mightier works unknown,
A style, a manner, and a fate their own.

   We, who for longer fame with labour strive,
Are pain'd to keep our sickly works alive;
Studious we toil, with patient care refine,
Nor let our love protect one languid line.
Severe ourselves, at last our works appear,
When, ah! we find our readers more severe;
For, after all our care and pains, how few
Acquire applause, or keep it if they do!
Not so these sheets, ordain'd to happier fate,
Praised through their day, and but that day their date;
Their careless authors only strive to join
As many words as make an even line;
As many lines as fill a row complete;
As many rows as furnish up a sheet:
From side to side, with ready types they run,
The measure's ended, and the work is done;
Oh, born with ease, how envied and how blest!
Your fate to–day and your to–morrow's rest,
To you all readers turn, and they can look
Pleased on a paper, who abhor a book;
Those who ne'er deign'd their Bible to peruse,
Would think it hard to be denied their News;
Sinners and saints, the wisest with the weak,
Here mingle tastes, and one amusement seek;
This, like the public inn, provides a treat,
Where each promiscuous guest sits down to eat;
And such this mental food, as we may call
Something to all men, and to some men all.

   Next, in what rare production shall we trace
Such various subjects in so small a space?
As the first ship upon the waters bore

The Village and The Newspaper

Incongruous kinds who never met before;
Or as some curious virtuoso joins
In one small room, moths, minerals, and coins,
Birds, beasts, and fishes; nor refuses place
To serpents, toads, and all the reptile race;
So here compress'd within a single sheet,
Great things and small, the mean and mighty meet.
'Tis this which makes all Europe's business known,
Yet here a private man may place his own:
And, where he reads of Lords and Commons, he
May tell their honours that he sells rappee.

   Add next th' amusement which the motley page
Affords to either sex and every age:
Lo! where it comes before the cheerful fire,–
Damps from the press in smoky curls aspire
(As from the earth the sun exhales the dew),
Ere we can read the wonders that ensue:
Then eager every eye surveys the part
That brings its favourite subject to the heart;
Grave politicians look for facts alone,
And gravely add conjectures of their own:
The sprightly nymph, who never broke her rest
For tottering crowns or mighty lands oppress'd,
Finds broils and battles, but neglects them all
For songs and suits, a birth–day, or a ball:
The keen warm man o'erlooks each idle tale
For "Monies wanted," and "Estates on Sale;"
While some with equal minds to all attend,
Pleased with each part, and grieved to find an end.

   So charm the news; but we who, far from town,
Wait till the postman brings the packet down,
Once in the week, a vacant day behold,
And stay for tidings, till they're three days old:
That day arrives; no welcome post appears,
But the dull morn a sullen aspect wears:
We meet, but ah! without our wonted smile,

The Village and The Newspaper

To talk of headaches, and complain of bile;
Sullen we ponder o'er a dull repast,
Nor feast the body while the mind must fast.
   A master passion is the love of news,
Not music so commands, nor so the Muse:
Give poets claret, they grow idle soon;
Feed the musician and he's out of tune;
But the sick mind, of this disease possess'd,
Flies from all cure, and sickens when at rest.
   Now sing, my Muse, what various parts compose
These rival sheets of politics and prose.
   First, from each brother's hoard a part they draw,
A mutual theft that never feared a law;
Whate'er they gain, to each man's portion fall,
And read it once, you read it through them all:
For this their runners ramble day and night,
To drag each lurking deed to open light;
For daily bread the dirty trade they ply,
Coin their fresh tales, and live upon the lie:
Like bees for honey, forth for news they spring,—
Industrious creatures! ever on the wing;
Home to their several cells they bear the store,
Cull'd of all kinds, then roam abroad for more.
   No anxious virgin flies to "fair Tweed–side;"
No injured husband mourns his faithless bride;
No duel dooms the fiery youth to bleed;
But through the town transpires each vent'rous deed.
Should some fair frail one drive her prancing pair
Where rival peers contend to please the fair;
When, with new force, she aids her conquering eyes,
And beauty decks, with all that beauty buys:
Quickly we learn whose heart her influence feels,
Whose acres melt before her glowing wheels.
   To these a thousand idle themes succeed,
Deeds of all kinds, and comments to each deed.
Here stocks, the state barometers, we view,

The Village and The Newspaper

That rise or fall by causes known to few;
Promotion's ladder who goes up or down;
Who wed, or who seduced, amuse the town;
What new–born heir has made his father blest;
What heir exults, his father now at rest;
That ample list the Tyburn–herald gives,
And each known knave, who still for Tyburn lives.
  So grows the work, and now the printer tries
His powers no more, but leans on his allies.
  When lo! the advertising tribe succeed,
Pay to be read, yet find but few will read;
And chief th' illustrious race, whose drops and pills
Have patent powers to vanquish human ills:
These, with their cures, a constant aid remain,
To bless the pale composer's fertile brain;
Fertile it is, but still the noblest soil
Requires some pause, some intervals from toil;
And they at least a certain ease obtain
From Katterfelto's skill, and Graham's glowing strain.
  I too must aid, and pay to see my name
Hung in these dirty avenues to fame;
Nor pay in vain, if aught the Muse has seen,
And sung, could make these avenues more clean;
Could stop one slander ere it found its way,
And give to public scorn its helpless prey.
By the same aid, the Stage invites her friends,
And kindly tells the banquet she intends;
Thither from real life the many run,
With Siddons weep, or laugh with Abingdon;
Pleased in fictitious joy or grief, to see
The mimic passion with their own agree;
To steal a few enchanted hours away
From self, and drop the curtain on the day.
  But who can steal from self that wretched wight
Whose darling work is tried some fatal night?
Most wretched man! when, bane to every bliss,

The Village and The Newspaper

He hears the serpent–critic's rising hiss;
Then groans succeed; nor traitors on the wheel
Can feel like him, or have such pangs to feel.
Nor end they here: next day he reads his fall
In every paper; critics are they all:
He sees his branded name with wild affright,
And hears again the cat–calls of the night.
    Such help the STAGE affords: a larger space
Is fill'd by PUFFS and all the puffing race.
Physic had once alone the lofty style,
The well–known boast, that ceased to raise a smile:
Now all the province of that tribe invade,
And we abound in quacks of every trade.
    The simple barber, once an honest name,
Cervantes founded, Fielding raised his fame:
Barber no more—a gay perfumer comes,
On whose soft cheek his own cosmetic blooms;
Here he appears, each simple mind to move,
And advertises beauty, grace, and love.
"Come, faded belles, who would your youth renew,
And learn the wonders of Olympian dew;
Restore the roses that begin to faint,
Nor think celestial washes vulgar paint;
Your former features, airs, and arts assume,
Circassian virtues, with Circassian bloom.
Come, battered beaux, whose locks are turned to gray,
And crop Discretion's lying badge away;
Read where they vend these smart engaging things,
These flaxen frontlets with elastic springs;
No female eye the fair deception sees,
Not Nature's self so natural as these."
    Such are their arts, but not confined to them,
The muse impartial most her sons condemn:
For they, degenerate! join the venal throng,
And puff a lazy Pegasus along:
More guilty these, by Nature less design'd

For little arts that suit the vulgar kind.
That barbers' boys, who would to trade advance,
Wish us to call them smart Friseurs from France:
That he who builds a chop–house, on his door
Paints "The true old original Blue Boar!"–

   These are the arts by which a thousand live,
Where Truth may smile, and Justice may forgive:–
But when, amidst this rabble rout, we find
A puffing poet to his honour blind;
Who slily drops quotations all about
Packet or post, and points their merit out;
Who advertises what reviewers say,
With sham editions every second day;
Who dares not trust his praises out of sight,
But hurries into fame with all his might;
Although the verse some transient praise obtains,
Contempt is all the anxious poet gains.

   Now Puffs exhausted, Advertisements past,
Their Correspondents stand exposed at last;
These are a numerous tribe, to fame unknown,
Who for the public good forego their own;
Who volunteers in paper–war engage,
With double portion of their party's rage:
Such are the Bruti, Decii, who appear
Wooing the printer for admission here;
Whose generous souls can condescend to pray
For leave to throw their precious time away.

   Oh! cruel WOODFALL! when a patriot draws
His gray–goose quill in his dear country's cause,
To vex and maul a ministerial race,
Can thy stern soul refuse the champion place?
Alas! thou know'st not with what anxious heart
He longs his best–loved labours to impart;
How he has sent them to thy brethren round,
And still the same unkind reception found:
At length indignant will he damn the state,

Turn to his trade, and leave us to our fate.
   These Roman souls, like Rome's great sons, are known
To live in cells on labours of their own.
Thus Milo, could we see the noble chief,
Feeds, for his country's good, on legs of beef:
Camillus copies deeds for sordid pay,
Yet fights the public battles twice a–day:
E'en now the godlike Brutus views his score
Scroll'd on the bar–board, swinging with the door:
Where, tippling punch, grave Cato's self you'll see,
And *Amor Patriæ* vending smuggled tea.
   Last in these ranks, and least, their art's disgrace,
Neglected stand the Muses' meanest race;
Scribblers who court contempt, whose verse the eye
Disdainful views, and glances swiftly by:
This Poet's Corner is the place they choose,
A fatal nursery for an infant Muse;
Unlike that Corner where true Poets lie,
These cannot live, and they shall never die;
Hapless the lad whose mind such dreams invade,
And win to verse the talents due to trade.
   Curb then, O youth! these raptures as they rise,
Keep down the evil spirit and be wise;
Follow your calling, think the Muses foes,
Nor lean upon the pestle and compose.
   I know your day–dreams, and I know the snare
Hid in your flow'ry path, and cry "Beware!"
Thoughtless of ill, and to the future blind,
A sudden couplet rushes on your mind;
Here you may nameless print your idle rhymes,
And read your first–born work a thousand times;
Th'infection spreads, your couplet grows apace,
Stanzas to Delia's dog or Celia's face:
You take a name; Philander's odes are seen,
Printed, and praised, in every magazine:
Diarian sages greet their brother sage,

And your dark pages please th' enlightened age.–
Alas! what years you thus consume in vain,
Ruled by this wretched bias of the brain!
   Go! to your desks and counters all return;
Your sonnets scatter, your acrostics burn;
Trade, and be rich; or, should your careful sires
Bequeath your wealth, indulge the nobler fires;
Should love of fame your youthful heart betray,
Pursue fair fame, but in a glorious way,
Nor in the idle scenes of Fancy's painting stray.
   Of all the good that mortal men pursue,
The Muse has least to give, and gives to few;
Like some coquettish fair, she leads us on,
With smiles and hopes, till youth and peace are gone.
Then, wed for life, the restless wrangling pair
Forget how constant one, and one how fair:
Meanwhile Ambition, like a blooming bride,
Brings power and wealth to grace her lover's side;
And though she smiles not with such flattering charms,
The brave will sooner win her to their arms.
   Then wed to her, if Virtue tie the bands,
Go spread your country's fame in hostile lands;
Her court, her senate, or her arms adorn,
And let her foes lament that you were born:
Or weigh her laws, their ancient rights defend,
Though hosts oppose, be theirs and Reason's friend;
Arm'd with strong powers, in their defence engage,
And rise the THURLOW of the future age.

Footnotes:

{1} Lord Robert Manners, killed in battle April 1782.

Printed in the United Kingdom
by Lightning Source UK Ltd.
117048UKS00001B/67